Black & White Magic

by
Marie Laveau

other books available
from International imports:

Prayer Book
Powers of The Psalms
Candle Burning Magic
Devotions to The Saints
Secrets of Magical Seals
The Modern Herbal Spellbook
Modern Witchcraft Spellbook
Golden Secrets of Mystic Oils
Magic With Incense and Powders
Spellcraft, Hexcraft & Witchcraft
Voodoo Handbook of Cult Secrets
Your Lucky Number ... Forever
How to Conduct a Seance

INTERNATIONAL IMPORT
www.indioproducts.com

Copyright © 1991
Reprint 2012

Occult Books – Curios – Supplies

ISBN 0-943832-22-5

SPIRITISM

Divination, the foretelling of future events or the discovery of things secret or obscure by alleged converse with supernatural powers.

Rely upon yourself and learn to use your judgment in every detail of your daily life. You have free will and freedom of choice, and if you do not exercise them the responsibility is yours-and it is one which can-not be evaded. Realize the power of your mind, however little it is, and begin to use it consciously and firmly without a minute's delay. The Power of your Mind is as real and actual a force as the power of your hand. That which your mind pictures clearly, and your will demands strongly and untiringly, you can draw to you and make your own, sooner or later. No argument is necessary to convince you of the accuracy of this statement, for you can see it working out continually and exactly around you as you go through life.

Try to realize the power of your mind. Realize your Mind-realize your consciousness. Then, choose wisely, concentrate your Mind steadily and strongly upon what you have chosen until you have made it your own.

Be very sure that what you desire will be for your benefit-because if you are sincere and strong and persistent in using this great natural force of yours you will most certainly draw to yourself exactly what you have imagined and that which you have resolved to acquire.

Concentrate your Mind-power steadily and strongly upon your desire. Demand, and you will receive.

To the power of Mind may be attributed the extraordinary phenomena produced by "mediums" who profess to be in touch with the spirit world. The phenomena actually do occur, and those who are responsible for them are quite possibly unaware of the nature of their own powers. The levitation of tables without contact, for instance, has been proved beyond all doubt by the evidence of men of science whose names have a world-wide renown. But, on the Malabar coast, the home of Indian Magic. I have seen a magician-one who practiced the "pretended" art of magic-stretch himself upon a cot brought out from the servants' quarters, and in broad daylight, by sheer Mind-force raise that cot four to six inches from the ground, so that a lath or stick could he passed freely under the legs of it. That was claimed to be Magic.

It is generally admitted-and deplored-that the most successful mediums are ill-educated, and sometimes quite illiterate. It would be indeed strange if departed spirits should deliberately elect to manifest them-selves through such unworthy vehicles, but it is not at all strange that these people should be capable of exerting their Mind-forces to such an extraordinary degree. Having discovered their natural powers, they concentrate upon the developing of them to the exclusion of all else, unhampered (and uncontrolled) by the influences of education. It is a fact that in highly- educated people, Mind is sometimes impotent through non-use.

Until now no book has been at the disposal of the vast and ever-increasing numbers of those who are eager to study the science of Mind, Psychic forces and its tremendous power.

In writing this book, it is the aim of the writer to bring together all of the history and activities of Marie Laveau, who for a long number of years was known as the Hoo Doo Queen of New Orleans and whose fame spread all over the South and then penetrated the North of these United States of America.

She was known, feared, and loved by both whites and colored in her home city, called on her for advice by people in all walks of life.

Many whites believed in her and her peculiar religious activities and many scoffed and laughed at her, but she was a power among the colored who swore by her and practiced her rites and ceremonies, who, endeavoring to influence the course of events to their immediate benefit, brought their woes, their troubles and their hope of happiness to her for solution.

Many ancient rites can be traced down from the Old Egyptian Sorcerers, thence the Arabian semi-civilization through to Africa being brought to America by the slaves, who practiced the rites in a more or less original mariner according to their present surroundings.

The author claims no original procedures but merely chronicles things that have been done by this peculiar belief and the purposes for which they have been done, giving no advice and leaving the thinker to think for him or herself as to what to believe or not to believe, whether there is really any basis in fact or whether Marie Laveau was a great psychologist working by the power of her spirituality to accomplish such things as she has. In any event this book will be some addition to the ways and means of other days and may give a little light to the modern psychologist, spiritualists and other modern beliefs.

It is authentic history that Marie Laveau at one time was consulted by the Queen of England on a very important matter and after successfully accomplishing the orders of the Queen she was made a present of a very valuable and unique shawl besides the gift of a large sum of money.

Hoping the perusal will interest you and be of some benefit.

BIVINS, N. D. P.

NOTE

In presenting this revised edition of research works of many assumed authority in the Occult Arts, Black Magic, White Magic, Talismanic and others, the aim of the author is to bring out in a comprehensive way this type of cult belief which has been in practice since time immemorial and still holds sway among a large population in every country in the world.

The promotion or undue influence in advocating superstition is entirely disclaimed by the author, and he also does not assume responsibility for an action on the part of the reader.

HELPING HAND FOR PERSON WHO HAS NEVER HAD SPIRITUAL HELP

O Good Mother I come to you with tears in my eyes and a heart as heavy as steel. My whole life is full of regret for the many years that I have wasted and all of the sorrows I have undergone because of my own ignorance. All around me others have reaped the goodness that life has had to offer, while I have only had misery and sorrow. I beg of you dear Mother to help me to overcome all the years that I have neglected my spiritual life. Believe me, Dear Mother that the fault was not mine alone, as I had no one to guide me, no one to advise me. Without your help, Dear Mother I see an endless life of hopeless sorrow. Humbly, I beg you Dear Mother, to lift me from my knees and lead me to the path of spiritual growth and everlasting hope.

My dear child, of all the pleas that come to my ears, yours touches me most deeply, for truly it is most pitiful that a bleeding heart, yearning for help knows not which way to turn. How you must have suffered, groping in the darkness for spiritual help and understanding, knowing fear and uncertainty at its utmost.

But fear no longer my dear child, for happiness is within your grasp, but we must start from the beginning to help you build your mind, body and home to the highest possible level. And when we do these things, let us not forget the unhappy times and the people around us who still need a helping hand spiritually. For each time we help another person we advance on our own ladder of happiness.

First you will obtain a Lucky Hand, containing a Lode Stone, Black Cat Bone, and the lucky roots and herbs including the Mojo Bean. This you will anoint with the Master Oil every Friday and you will carry it with you wherever you go for protection and a spiritual uplift. You will put 20 drops of the Oil #20 in your bath at least once a week or more often if needed. Once a month you will cover your whole body with the oil of Cipriano and leave it on for one half hour and then take a hot bath with your Oil #20. This is best done just before retiring. While in the hot bath, close your eyes and say the Lord's prayer. When you have dried thoroughly, powder your chest with the Uncrossing Powder. You will have the soundest most restful sleep you have ever had.

In the morning use more Uncrossing Powder on your chest and a little of your Master Oil as a perfume, saying Dear Lord, "Please Help Me." This puts your body in good shape. Then to get your house in good order you must clean it thoroughly, adding the Van Van Floor Wash to the scrub water. Then you must sprinkle the Divine Spray in each corner of the whole house, including cupboards. The Jinx Removing Salt you sprinkle outside your front and back door. Have an all purpose candle burning for you at all times, so that whenever you think of it you will remember to thank the Lord for all your blessings.

My dear child these things you will do to start yourself upward to spiritual heights you did not believe possible. After these things have been done you are now in a position to work on any condition that you desire. God bless you.

SO BE IT.

GOING TO TRIAL

O my daughter you come to me in your trials and tribulations and say unto me 0 good mother I am sore of feet and heavy of heart, for the power of man has said that I shall be put in the darkest dungeon and that I shall he deprived of the beauty, pleasures and good will of the world, that my friend shall look down on me and that they shall show displeasure and pass me with their faces turned away.

That my enemies will vilify me and say untruths, blasphemy, and perjure me, to my dismay, so that they can point their fingers at me and pass me in the streets of the city and on the head of those dear to me and those who love me.

O daughter I say unto you that you shall come before the judges and the scribes and your law man will pass judgment upon you and according to your faith and hope, so you shall be judged and according to your sacrifices and invocations, you shall be judged and according to the wise counsels and smooth tongues so shall you be judged.

O daughter to cool the wrath of God you shall take some of the root of the John the Conqueror and upon it you shall sprinkle ten drops of the essence of Bend Over and you shall wrap it in a piece of red flannel and you shall place it behind your bed. There it shall remain for nine days. At the same time you shall burn one Devotional Candle for each of the nine days. At the end of the nine days you shall take the root from behind the bed and place it in your pocket until the day that you go to trial, allowing no one to touch it but yourself. For nine days before going to court add one teaspoon Dragon Blood Bath to your bath water each day, anoint yourself with Master Oil.

On the day of the trial you shall take a new, dry piece of root of the John the Conqueror and chew it as you enter the court room and you shall spit the finely chewed root inside of the court room, allowing no one to see you do it. And on the day that the judges shall call you to trial, you shall obey them taking with you, your man of law and your witness. And the judges shall listen to the testimony of your friends, and hear with you and believe you, and he shall deal with you mildly.

THE PERSON WHO WISHED TO BE UNCROSSED

O my child you come unto me and say, good mother my house has been crossed and confusion reigns, where there should be peace, words of bitter regret are spoken, where there should be words of praise, words of jealousy and doubt, where there should be words of love, only words of strife and crossed purposes, where only confidence and good will should be found.

My dear ones look with suspicion on me and strangers hearken not to my voice, neither do they believe my words even when spoken with respect and truth.

The stranger leaves my house in anger, my loved ones do not come to comfort me, I am desolate, uncared for, unloved and miserable. Oh my good mother I pray you to look with favor on your broken spirited daughter and help me in my troubles, fill my house with good spirits, give cheer and comfort where there is only strife.

Oh my good mother make the stranger speak to me with a sweet voice, make them believe in me, make them hearken to my words that I may have my way with them.

O my daughter when your house is crossed and you find no happiness in it, it is decreed that you shall take root of "King Solomon" and place it in a glass full of "Water of Notre Dame" and keep it in your house for three days. On the fourth day you shall sprinkle the water in every corner of your house, making sure that no eyes watch you do this and you shall burn the "John the Conqueror Incense" every day so that the smoke thereof will drive away the evil spirits and leave only the good spirits. And you shall take the essence of "Van Van Floor Wash" and scrub the wood work and floors of your house. Each day, for seven days you will add to your bath water the Seven Day Uncrossing Bath. On your arms, legs and chest you will rub yourself with a few drops of the Uncrossing Oil. On your shoulders and chest you will powder yourself with the Uncrossing Powder. And as the sun falls low in the heavens you shall sprinkle yourself with the essence of "Jockey Club" and when you meet your loved ones and your friends and your relatives at the door you will meet them with a clear face and honest words and you will sympathize with them, and they will bring you cheer and the evil spirits shall be conquered and the evil spirits shall remain away from your place and only the good spirits will remain.

After nine days you will burn nine green candles (Blessed) at the rate of one a day and you shall have great care that no ill-will quench their flame.

SO BE IT.

THE LADY WHO WISHED TO CROSS HER ENEMIES

Oh good mother I come to you with my heart bowed down and my shoulders drooping and my spirits broken. For an enemy has sorely tried me. Has caused my loved ones to leave me, has taken from my worldly goods and my gold. Has spoken meanly of me and caused my friends to lose their faith in me. On my knees I pray to you O good mother that you will cause confusion to reign in my enemies house and that you will cause hatred to be on my enemies head and that you will take their power from them and cause them to be unsuccessful.

Oh my daughter I have heard your woes, and your pains and tribulation and in the depth of the wisdom of the Gods I will help you to find peace and happiness.

My dear daughter it is written that you shall take some Four Thieves Vinegar, pour it into a shallow plate and dip into it a sheet of pressed parchment paper and when it has been well soaked, take it out and let it dry, then you will write upon this paper the name of your enemy with the Blood of the Doves. Then you will hold this paper in the flame of the Black Wax Double Action Candle that has been rubbed with the Black Art Oil, until every bit of it has turned into ashes, then you will take the ashes and sprinkle it in front of your enemies house after sun-down.

After the lapse of three nights, you will take the Water of Mars, called War Water and in front of the house of your enemy, you will sprinkle it after sun-down. This you will do as you pass by, making sure that no one will see you in this act.

In your own house you will burn the John the Conqueror Incense every day and on the outside of your house on its four sides you shall sprinkle the Peace powder.

You will do all this so that you may control your enemies and take all of the power to harm you away from them.

Oh daughter, go in peace and do the work required of you so that you may have rest and comfort from your enemies and they will have no power to harm you in the sight of your friends and loved ones by their stinging tongues.

SO BE IT.

THE LADY WHO LOST HER LOVER

Oh my daughter you come unto me and say, good mother, the man of my heart has left me, he does not come to my house and tell me of his love. He passes me by without any smile on his face. His eyes no longer sparkle with love when he speaks to me. His heart is cold to all of my advances. He has eyes for other women, I have no longer the power to hold his tender thoughts. He listens to the voices of the siren and does not harken unto me. Oh good mother I come unto you in deep distress and poor in spirit, I beg for your help that I may be comforted and loved just as in the days gone by, and that my loved one may re-main by my side, for all of the beauty and sunshine has gone from my life.

My poor downcast daughter, it is with deep feeling and regret that I hear of your great pains and tribulations, but it is written that the sun shall again shine for you in gladness, and to accomplish this great desire, you will take the perfume of Van Van and upon your clothes you shall sprinkle three drops each day for fifteen days and two drops each day thereafter. Each day in your bath you shall put a few drops of the Oil #20. You shall take the Come To Me Powder and use it on your bosom and neck every day after washing or bathing. In your (Blessed) and before them you will pray that your charms will cause your loved one to think deeply of you and that you shall never be absent from his mind. Under each candle you shall place a piece of Pure Parchment Paper on which his name has been written with Pure Doves Blood. And you shall allow the wax to cover the name on the paper so that no one will see the name. And when he comes to you, you shall not reproach or insult him or speak to him of his past, but on the contrary, treat him kindly. You shall smile on him and you shall be friendly and true to him. You will do all of these things and you will be of good cheer and pure in purpose so that the Gods shall smile on your work and that your life shall be only beauty and sunshine.

THE LADY WHOSE HUSBAND OR MAN FRIEND LEFT HOME

Oh good mother I come unto you in deep distress and tears have coursed my face in the dark hours of the night, for he who was flesh of my Flesh, the blood of my heart and the companion of my soul. My dear husband has left our home and gone from my side, gone in the wilderness where my cries of distress will not reach him, where my tender words will not he heard by him, where the sirens and bad women will have sway over him and will make him forget me forever. He is gone where I cannot minister unto him, where I cannot show my love. He has left me desolate and where darkness closes in and about me and drags me down to the depths.

Oh good mother I cannot live without him, am sorely pressed and only ask for death without your help.

Oh my good daughter do not lose hope and faith for the stars say that there is a way to make your loved one's spirit commune with you and have him come back to your side, there to remain and to comfort and protect you, and in order to bring this about, and to bring your troubles to the attention of the good spirits and to get their help that they will stop the work of the spirits of ill omen against you, so that you will again find happiness.

You will bring into your home a Magnetic Horse Shoe that is red in the center and bright on the ends, and you will get of the Gold Magnetic Sand and this you will pour on the bright ends of the Magnetic Horse Shoe so that some will stick to it, this you will do to attract his love again and his worldly goods shall remain with you.

You will burn nine Pink Candles with his name under each one so that they will be for him only. You will burn them, one each day, before the sun goes down. And you will us the Drawing Powder every day on your neck and throat after bathing or washing.

And if he has not come, you will write him a good letter and in this letter you will sprinkle some Squint Drops so that he will have eyes only for you and so that he will not see the charms of other women. Nor will he listen to them or love them.

If for reasons known to you only, you wish he should become jealous of you and that Jealousy shall be to your advantage, it is written that you shall burn nine Devotional Candles, one each night For nine nights, these will make the green eyed monster of jealousy enter his mind and he will think of you both night and day and he shall stay awake in the dark hours of the night and think of you.

Fail not to do this for your happiness as your love depend upon it.

SO BE IT.

THE LADY WHO HAS AN EMPTY HOUSE

Oh good mother I come to you to ask your help, for prosperity and plenty is not for me. The stranger passes my door and sees me not, neither do they stop nor look into my house. My place is empty, there is no laughter nor is there any feast days, for they know me not, on the dark days nor on the feast days, neither do they remember me or know me.

The clink of gold has not passed my palm for many days, neither friends nor strangers have brought me gifts, my purse hangs limp from my tassel with no hopes of having it filled.

Oh good mother I am full of lamentations and the evil spirits live in my house so I beg that you shall hear my prayer and in the fullness of your wisdom give me help.

My poor helpless daughter, in the fullness of my heart I will help you to make prosperity smile on you that you will have again feast days and that your friends will remember you always and be at your side and that your raiment shall be of many hues and fine texture and that it shall reflect your prosperity.

In front of each room of your house you will sprinkle the Silver Magnetic Sand and you will put into your scrub water on the days that you dress up your house at the end of the week, Friday being the best day, some Van Van Floor Wash and with this you will clean the floors and closets of your house and you will burn every day the John the Conqueror Incense, the ashes of which you will throw in your back yard after each burning. You will use on your hands and arms the Compelling Oil and on your neck the Easy Life Oil.

And you shall sprinkle on your clothes each day three drops of the Nine Lucky Mixture that it may keep your spirit gay and never to die.

Do all of these things so that the men folks shall enter and be entertained and that they shall remain pleased with you and shall shower you with kindness and worldly goods and prosperity shall enter and drive away care and worry.

SO BE IT.

THE PERSON WHOSE BUSINESS IS IN BAD SHAPE

Oh good mother your daughter comes to you on bended knees to ask for a great favor. For where there was light and laughter now there is only silence, where many feet wore out the threshold of my front door. Now scarcely anyone enters, where gold crossed my palm in a steady stream not even a shekel is now seen. No gold or silver or worldly goods come to me. My goods remain in my store house, with no one to buy or even ask the price thereof. So good mother if I do not soon get help and if you do not hear my prayer the sheriff and his minions will soon enter my household and my store house and take from me what I have left to sell.

Oh my daughter it is said that she who has, more again shall be given. So to make that come to pass you will take some Steel Dust and some Drawing Powder. This you will mix together and separate them into four parts and you will put one of them in each of the four corners of the room wherein the business is done, this is said by the spirits to make the mind follow your goods and chattels so that the stranger will buy from you that which you have to sell, or if professional, will increase the business and money will again pass the palm of your hands.

And you will put into the water with which you wash the floor of your business place fifteen drops of the Van Van Floor Wash, and with this you will scrub the floor of your business place every Friday and before the doors are opened in the morning you shall burn of the John the Conqueror Incense every day. In each room, every corner, including closets and cupboards sprinkle the Divine Spray, so that undesirable vibrations will find it impossible to stay. This you will do so that faith will enter in company with good luck and the spirit of contention and strife will leave.

Herein fail not my daughter to do faithfully each of these things so that prosperity shall again smile on you and so that strangers and friends will come unto you and say, "Lo I am much pleased with you and I will come again.

Let the music begin for I am satisfied in my business dealings with you.

SO BE IT.

TO STOP GOSSIP

Oh good mother I am now before you that you may judge, for my lady friends have spoken my name from the house tops and from the hills and they have attacked my character and questioned my virtue. They have said jealous things of me and caused my name to become a byword among the people.

Oh good mother I have to hang my head when I pass the friend or the stranger for I know not the viper tongue has reached them and that scandal and untruths have been called to their attention, and that they have heard dark stories and low sayings about me. Tears are in my eyes and my lips tremble. Oh mother help your humble daughter.

Dear child, you who worship at the shrine, my aching heart and my pity is for you, so that I will again make the flush of pride brighten up your cheeks and laughter come into your eyes where there is now only tears, and I will make it that you walk with your head unbowed, to look all in the face, and in order to accomplish this work you will do:

When you speak to the stranger and to the friend, you will chew a piece of John the Conqueror Root so that your words will sound sweet and they will turn their minds toward you. These chewed roots you will spit in front of the house of those who speak meanly of you.

And in your home you will burn the Sandal Wood Incense and while the fumes are rising from it, you stand in the center of the room looking towards the door that evil thoughts will leave your house just as the fumes are slowly vanishing and leave you clear of all evil spirits. This you will do for nine days without fail and with prayers on your lips.

Pour one teaspoonful of "Uncrossing Bath" in the water in which you bathe. In every corner of your house you shall sprinkle the Water of Peace. All these things you will faithfully do so that the tongue of the viper shall be everlastingly stilled so that scandals and jealousies shall die and in its place shall live only great joy and happiness.

SO BE IT.

13

HOW TO PROMOTE PEACE IN THE HOME

My friend, you come to me with tears in your eyes and worried over the condition of your home. Where there should be harmony, love, understanding and peace, only sadness and disappointment fill the atmosphere.

It is my advice, dear friend, that you follow these instructions and bring sunshine into your home.

Sprinkle every room of your house with "Peace Water" and burn the "John the Conqueror Incense" mixed with the "Helping Hand Incense". Sprinkle some "Jinx Removing Salt" all around the outside of your house.

Apply to your body daily the "Peace Powder" and anoint your head and clothes with "Bend Over Drops".

Burn for one hour each day or night the "Peace Candle" until you have burned three of them.

Do these things, my dear child, and let no frown be reflected on your face.

Peace be with you.

SO BE IT.

THE LADY WHO CANNOT GET FRIENDS

Oh good mother the evil spirit seems to completely envelop me, I have no attraction, no sympathy from my kind, my lady friends look on me with indifference, their friendship is only luke-warm, their sympathy for me has fled. I ask them and they promise, but they do not do as I ask. I invite them and they say yes but they do not come. They pass me by in the market place and bow to me sometimes, but more often they look me not in the face. They stop to speak to others, but when I approach there is no more to speak about and everything becomes quiet, so I seem to have lost the power to hold my friendship. They look with the eyes and they see me not, they speak with the lips, but their words are empty and of no value.

0 my daughter, you have truly lost your spirit and your words to your friends do not ring true, so they believe you not. You have lost your magnetism, so your actions do not attract others to you. Look well to yourself first and take heed that you try to value your friends, for the spirits have said that she who wishes to get back her power to attract must use on her body the Attraction Powder after bathing. And in the far corner of the drawer where clothes are kept a piece of the John the Conqueror root shall be placed. On your neck and ears you will use the Master Oil.

And in your house there shall be cheerfulness and no evil thoughts. And you will keep this spirit of cheer in your house by scrubbing the floors with water in which a few drops of the "Van Van Floor Wash" have been mixed. And in your bath you shall pour ten drops of the "Oil of Lavender" and a handful of table salt, so that you will welcome any kind of good company.

Oh daughter do you always think faithfully and depart in peace.

SO BE IT.

THE LADY WHO CANNOT KEEP MEN FRIENDS

Oh good mother, I pray you to judge me and give me advice, for my men friends do not smile on me. They meet me and see me not, they do not speak to me in the warm words of friendship, they forget me even as I pass, they do not even remember my name. When I go to the feast I sit near the wall unadorned and uncalled for. They have no bright sayings for me and care not to incur my favor so I remain forlorn and forsaken while all about me is laughter and good fellowship. Lo. I am with them, but not of them.

When I speak to them to come to my house to visit me, neither do they say yes, nor do they say no. If they come they make no effort to entertain me, nor to make me care-free or mirthful, they speak to me only in a cool and distant manner.

Dear daughter, I have heard your words of trouble and sympathize with you, and in order that your bright star will shine again and that your mind will prevail you will do the following things faithfully:

In your bath water you should pour 10 drops of Special Oil No. 20.

You will every day after bathing use on your bosom and neck the French Love Powder and in your purse you will carry the Heart of the Swallow, this combination will serve to attract even that which you have lost. In the east corner of the room where you sleep, there you shall burn for one hour each day, the Blessed Pink Love Candle and while it burns, you shall stand in Front of it for five minutes and think of him whom you love.

And in your house you will burn each day the Lucky John the Conqueror Incense to eliminate the forces that are working against you. You will make sure that its smoke will reach every corner of the house. By doing this you will absorb good vibration and your friends will meet you with cheerful faces. They will remain with you as you wish.

SO BE IT.

THE LADY OR MAN IN THE LAW SUIT

Oh good mother I am on my knees before you to pray for help as I am deeply troubled and persecuted by my enemies. They say unto the judge, lo this woman has broken the law, she has made war on us and caused disturbances in our family. Another one says, oh most learned judge, this woman has taken weapons of war and has attempted to spill my life's blood, and still another one says to the High Sheriff, oh sir, I pray you to help me for this woman has taken my worldly goods and has entered my house when I was away doing my labor in the fields.

Oh good Mother, now the learned judge and the high sheriff and the men of the law have threatened to put me in the dungeon where there is no light and the vermin crawl over you and eat out your heart, where only gloom will be my companion, where I will never see the face of the sun. Oh good Mother help your downtrodden daughter.

My poor daughter I hear your prayer and will hasten to your help with heartfelt sympathy and tell you the secrets of the learned judges and the high priests so that you can conquer your enemies and once more breathe the air of freedom, so that the sun shall shine on your head and bring you comfort, so that the good moon shall bring you peace and smiles on your face.

You shall take the herb of Five Finger Grass and the essence of Geranium and put them together and wrap them up in a piece of red flannel and when the low sheriff serves you with paper, you shall fold it in four parts and in it the flannel with the geranium and the Five Finger Grass and place it for two nights under your bed that the power to soothe the anger of the law will be worked on it until the time when you shall come before the judge, and in your house you shall sprinkle in every corner the water of peace called Peace Water, and you will have in your purse the John Conqueror Root and you will allow no one to touch it until your troubles shall be over with.

And the night before you are to appear before the judges you will burn three Peace Candles, and the John the Conqueror Incense, mixed with Helping-Hand Incense. This so that the testimony of your enemy will not be believed by the learned judge and the high sheriff and so that he will become confused when he speaks to the judge against you.

My child, do all of these things so that you can triumph over your enemies and have power and happiness.

SO BE IT.

THE GAMBLING HAND

Great Goddess of Chance I would ask your favor, I would ask for pieces of gold and pieces of silver from your hand, for when I go to the race course the horses do not heed me or make strong efforts that I may be victor and the driver of the chariot does not lash his steeds that they may come on the first line, but instead lag behind that I may lose my gold and my silver.

When I pray to you with the dice in my hands, you do not smile on me, neither do you guide the dice that they may show a smiling face to me, but instead you guide them that they may turn to help the other players and I go home with my pockets empty and my heart heavy.

So again when I sit me down among the select men and play with them the game of cards, you do not put into my hands the cards which will undo my opponents, but instead you put into the hand of the other players the high cards which will make them my masters.

Tell me, oh great Goddess of Chance, what can I do to appease your anger and win your approving smile, that I may wax fat and have unto my purse the bright gold and jingling silver of the empire. I am your steadfast worshipper and would first win your favor, so that my horses shall come to the visors line the first ones, and so that the dice will be friendly to me, so that the high cards shall burn to get into my hands.

My son, you have asked a great favor of me, but you have not burned any incense at my altar and have not made any offering to my spirit, for I look only with favor on those who are my steadfast worshippers, for those who come for a day, I know them not, neither do I smile on them. But for those who worship at my shrine I smile on them. For those of good spirit I love them, an if you wish to receive my favor, you will put into a small bag made of red flannel the following worshipful and holy articles: The John the Conqueror Root, the powder of the magnetic stone, called Magnetic Powder, the Black Cat Bone and the Lode Stone. These you will close tightly in the bag so that they will not leak out, and on the day you care to win, you will put on this bag three drops of the Cleo May and carry in your left pocket and let no one touch it. And on your hands when you are playing with the dice or the cards you will rub the essence called the Lucky Dog. And in your house you will burn the Incense of John the Conqueror.

Fail not to do this and you will enjoy good luck and happiness.

SO BE IT.

THE LUCKY HAND

Oh good Mother I come to you to lay at your feet my most deep trouble. It seems that everything that I may try to do goes against me. When I think that I have something with which I can gather pieces of gold and wax Fat and prosperous, lo it is but clay in my hands. I can get no encouragement from the women and men with whom I speak and I am turned a deaf ear so that they will not hear me. When I see a place with which I can succeed and put my gold into it, lo the customers do not come and they pass my door and do not even look around.

When I see good merchandise and good chattels which I can easily get and sell them at much profit, to when they come into my hands they are only dross and have no value. When I go to see the big chiefs and talk pleasantly to them, that I can do very many things to their advantage and will make them wax fat with riches, lo they turn their heads and will not even hear me.

So it is one failure after another, one disappointment after another and here I am on my knees before you with very few shekels and a very poor heart, so that my spirit is broken and I know not what to do, will you, oh good Mother, also turn me away empty handed and leave me in despair, I pray you that you will call upon the good spirits to help me, and take me as your own.

My child rise up and take heart, for those stout of heart and willing of hands I say that they shall not fail even if the evil spirits have conspired against them for I will lend my hand and my help and uphold them and make them strong again.

To accomplish this purpose you will take a small bag made of red flannel and in it you will put a piece of live Lode Stone and Lode Stone Dust and the root of John the Conqueror and the Black Cat Bone and the Eye of the Cat, this you will tie together in the bag and carry with you in a way that no one will touch it.

At the rise of the New Moon you will sprinkle on this bag three drops of the Master Oil and at the rise of the full moon you will sprinkle three drops of the Essence of Has No Hanna and you will say the following prayer in each occasion:

Oh good Lord make me stout of heart.
Oh good Lord let my sight penetrate the innermost things.
Oh good Lord give me power to speak.
Oh good Lord let my words be harkened to.
Oh good Lord drive the evil spirit from me.
Oh good Lord give me success.
Oh good Lord let me hold all of these things into this bag.
Oh good Lord never leave me.
and to my son this is the great secret of the Lucky Hand, put it where you can always come into contact with it. That will give you power and confidence in yourself and you can go forth without fear, and that all things must come to you and that you shall not know any such word as failure.

SO BE IT.

THE MAN WHOSE WIFE LEFT HIM

Oh god Mother, look into your son's upturned face and bear with him until he has told you of his trouble and sorrow and poured his tale of misery at your feet.

He comes to you for help and comfort knowing that in all your wisdom he can count on happiness if you so wish it.

Dear Mother, the woman of my heart has left my roof and I have no peace or rest She has gone from me with very few words and has left me broken-hearted for I have her always in my mind and can not sleep for her face is always before me and for the remembrance of all times when so many sweet words were spoken to each other and so many tender moments was passed in each other's company.

Tales have come to my ears that she has left me for another man who she loves better than she does me. Other tales are that she left because she does not love me any more, as she used to do in the long ago. I do not know what to do or what to believe. I come to you that you may quiet my mind and make her think of me often and make her come back to me and love me in the same old way as she did before.

My dear son, your heart-broken story has come to me and I hasten to answer your prayer that you may take your place again in the house of happiness, for love is at the bottom of all things and rules the world.

So in order that you may win back the love of your wife and in order that she will come back to you, you will do the following things:

In and around the house in which you dwelt in happiness with your woman you will sprinkle of the Gold Magnetic Sand, and if you still live in the same house, you will scrub the floor of your room with Oil of Rosemary and Oil of Verbena mixed together in equal portions, of this mixture you shall pour twenty drops in your scrubbing water, but if you have moved and you want her to follow you to your new home, then you will scrub your room with the Oil of Verbena and the Oil of Rosemary mixed together and of this mixture you shall pour twenty drops in your scrubbing water every Saturday.

And you will go to see her and upon your clothes you will sprinkle of the Essence of Has Na Hanna close to your body, and you will speak to her with sweet words and many promises, that she will believe you and follow you.

And if you cannot see her wherein she dwells now, then you will write her a letter of love and forgiveness and in that letter, you will put two drops of the Extract of Bend Over, so that she will read the words written therein and believe them. And in your house you will burn Nine Red Candles (Blessed), made of pure wax, one each night for nine nights so that the flames of love shall he rekindled and shall burn again, and under each of these candles, as they burn, you will put her name on pure Parchment Paper, so that the wax shall fall over it as the candles burn.

And to make her jealous of you, you will burn Nine Pure Wax Candles, but green in color, with the name of the one she is jealous of under it, written on pure parchment paper, this you will do for nine nights at the rate of one each night without intermission.

You may burn the red candle and the green candle at the same time if you choose, but in different corners of the room, and after you get her to come to you, you will then take the Love Powder and put it in her shoes or on her powder puff in a way that she will not see or notice it, this you will do to increase her love for you and that her mind will not change and that she will remain with you to her last day.

SO BE IT.

THE MAN WHO LOST HIS SWEETHEART

Oh dear Mother you see your son before you with tears in his eyes and a downcast look in his face for I have lost my beautiful sweetheart whom I have loved for many a day and whom I cannot forget. She is always in my mind and I cannot sleep for the thoughts of her even in the day time. In my fancy I see her just out of my reach, her beautiful form and face is always before me, night and day, in my waking hours and in my hours of labor.

I see no more her sweet smile when she received me, I hear not her sweet voice when she spoke to me, I would gladly give half my life for another moment of happiness with her such as there were many before.

Oh Mother will you hear my prayer and help me.

My poor son I hearken to your your words of sorrow and gladly extend my help that you may smile again the smile of happiness and that you will again be glad to see the streak of daylight break the skies, that your tears will stop their flow and you will be yourself again with your sweet-heart at your side. Lo, in order to bring about his great day, you will do exactly as the "MAN WHO LOST HIS WIFE" in the preceding chapter. After this has been thoroughly done and you come face to face with your sweetheart you will present her with a box of sweets, upon which she will smile and speak to you words of endearment and make you glad.

The Gold Magnetic Sand should be sprinkled around the place where you live, and the Essence of Rosemary and Verbena for scrubbing purpose should be used in your room, not where your sweetheart lives.

In your bath water you should pour 10 drops of special oil No. 20.

SO BE IT.

TO OBTAIN SUCCESS

Oh dear Mother, I come unto you to ask for your help. My mind and my spirit have been burdened to the breaking point. I beg of thee, oh dear Mother, to turn no deaf ears to my supplications that I may be successful in those things which I desire within the bounds of reason.

My dear child, I understand your tribulations and your trials, In order that you may accomplish the desires of your heavily burdened heart, you should start by burning for one hour each day two candles, one green and one red, side by side. In front of these candles you should stand and recite the 23rd Psalm one time, leaving the candles to burn the remainder of the hour.

Dust your body daily with "Algiers Powder" and anoint your head also daily with "Success Oil". Pour one half teaspoonful of "Dragon Mood Bath" into your bath water, together with ten drops of "Special Oil No. 20".

Do these things, my dear child, with faith and constancy and the spirit of success will smile at you. God bless you.

SO BE IT.

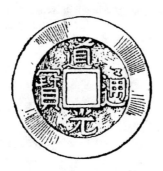

THE MAN WHO CANNOT GET A SWEETHEART

O dear Mother, I come unto you so that I can get some of your good and wholesome advice for I don't seem to have any luck or any chance to get a sweetheart. I see them once and speak sweetly to them and they seem to like my looks and harken unto my words, but lo when I go back the second time all of their encouragement seems to have gone, I meet them in parties and seem to have a very good time with them and make them joyous and happy, but when I speak of calling upon them they turn a deaf ear unto me.

I meet them socially and hi company and seem to be welcome, but when I wish to commune with them privately, lo their excuses are many and I can make no headway in my love affairs. Oh my good Mother my heart yearns for the love of a sweetheart and it would he my complete happiness if I could make them understand me and make them love me in return. Tell me, oh tell me, what has done this to me. When all of my friends are successful I am to be cast off and can find no place and no one to give my caresses to and talk of love to me.

My son I am glad you have come to me for advice, for many more good sons of mine who are beset with the same evil come not to me and therefore are not happy. You seem to be surrounded with the spirit of opposition and cannot make your way with the one you would love, so in order that you may he blessed you will do as follows; You will get of the Peace Water and sprinkle it in front of the house wherein lives the lady of your choice, sprinkle it in such a manner that she will step on it or over it.

You will do this for three nights after dark when no one will see you and be sure that you step over it when you go in to see her and before going in to see her, you will sprinkle on your garments the Love Drops. And on your skin you will use the Love Powder, so that she will listen to your words and tell her in words of love how beautiful she is and how sweet is her voice when she speaks and that you love to hear her words so that you will impress her mind that you really think very much of her.

And in the water in which you bathe you will sprinkle every day for three weeks five drops of the Black Cat Perfume so that you will attract to you the spirit of love and it will help you to gain over your desires. And in case you cannot see her or speak to her, then you will sit yourself down and write her a letter. In this letter you will praise her and speak of her beauty, and before you seal this letter you will put a few drops of the Jocky Club Perfume, all around the edge of the paper. And when you get so that you are well acquainted with her, but not before then, you will put some of the courting powder on her powder puff or in her shoes or on her garments so that her love for you will grow warmer and she will never turn from you or forget you. In your room you will burn of the John the Conqueror incense every day. So my son do all of these things to get the help of the God of Love, so that he will give you many happy days.

THE MAN WHOSE BUSINESS IS POOR

Oh dear Mother I pray come to my rescue as I am almost to my last resort and my last shekel, for all of my good business is gone from me and my pockets are no more heavy with the gold and silver like in the olden days.

My old friends who at one time came to me and were pleased with my goods are now gone from me. They pass my door and do not even look in.

All those who were glad to bid me the time and eagerly take my advice when they were in need of my goods, now believe me not. Once in a while when a stranger steps in my house of business it seems as if I cannot please them with my goods or with my sweet words, and lo they walk out empty-handed.

Where there was gay laughter and many pieces of silver changed hands, now we hear only silence. My goods remain on my shelves until they are spoiled and I cannot even get what the merchant prince has asked me to pay for them. So good Mother if I do not soon get help and bring once more the tinkle of silver to my purse I will be set upon by the money lenders and the sheriff and only woe will be my lot and gone will be my house of business. Good Mother I can only go to you for help, pray hear my cries of distress.

My good son I have heard your plea and I think that the God of Mamon will help you in your need and show you the way of good business and much customers, and also make some of your old customers come back to you to do as in the old days. You will have to pacify the Gods of Mamon as follows:

Take the Jinx Removing Sprinkling Salts and sprinkle it on the front part of your house or business. Place outside the door, that people may walk on or over it without noticing it, and when you have closed up for the night then you will burn the John the Conqueror Incense, mixed with the Good Luck Spiritual Incense, allowing the fumes to penetrate every corner of the place. And for yourself you will take of the root of John the Conqueror and put it in your pocket and when you get up in the. morning, before opening the door for business, the first thing you will do will be to put three drops of the Lucky Lode Stone Perfume of the John the Conqueror root, so that it will attract money and you will have the power of talking to your customers that they will buy your goods, but be sure that once you have made the John the Conqueror Root work for you, no other human hand shall touch it, but yours. So that the power of attraction shall be for you and no other.

And my child be sure that you treat your customers with due consideration and with honesty, and always have the kindness of your heart showing on your face so that the customer will come unto you and give you the confidence and respect.

Herein fail not as the God of Maroon will not continue to smile on you and give you gold and silver if you do not deed their advice for the Gods of Mamon have two heads and can speak good and evil at the same time.

SO BE IT.

TO CONTROL TROUBLESOME NEIGHBORS

Oh dear Mother I come unto you to tell you of my unsettled mind and my grave troubles. There is some one who lives near me, but who has no neighborly love for me nor any one else, but is only full of selfishness and of a mean mind and makes continual trouble for every one who lives close near and around me, so that there is a continuous strife and wailing wherever that person may be. When I pass near their place of living they at once utter mean words loud enough so that they will reach my ears, in order that I may stop and say to them mean words in return so that this will lead to a court scrape and that the men of the laws may interfere with me, also when any of my loved ones pass the place wherein they live. Then again slander reaches their ears so that there shall be no peace in the neighborhood. When anyone comes to visit the place where I live they lie in wait for them until they come out and words of blasphemy and reproach reach their ears. Can you not in your great wisdom tell me which evil spirit makes them successful in their work of the devil so that I may hope to protect my home and my loved ones and in the end attain peace of mind.

My dear son I hear your prayer and will hasten to enlighten you so that all things you have asked me for shall come to you; all things you wish for may become true.

It is the Spirit of Restlessness and envy that urges your neighbor to bother you and speak words which may cause trouble and war among your neighbors, and if you wish to placate this spirit it is necessary that you proceed as is commanded you.

You will take of the Hot Foot Powder and sprinkle of this powder at a place where your enemy will walk so that the fever to move will take hold of them and enter their body and they will become dissatisfied with their place of living and move away and not bother either you or your good neighbors any more.

And in your home, you will sprinkle the Peace Powder in every corner of your living room or bed room, so that the powder of the spirit of evil who controls your enemy will lose all of its strength to work against you and that there shall be peace in and around you.

And in your garments you will sprinkle of the Lucky John the Conqueror Perfume and the Master Oil every day. And you will burn the Lucky John the Conqueror Incense in your house every day so that the good forces may come and stay with you. After dark you will burn for one hour each night the Black Wax Candle, this will torment the mind of the ones you wish to move until they cannot rest in peace, and will take their departure.

Be sure that you yourself treat your neighbors in the spirit of peace and righteousness and that your tongue shall be stilled of everything but kindness and that your mind will generate nothing but sweet and pure thoughts. Do these things and win.

SO BE IT.

HOW TO DEVELOP HAPPINESS

It is important, my dear child, to understand that certain amount of sacrifice is very important in your journey through life in order to attain the highest degree of happiness. How to stand the pains and suffering of the mind and body, and to finally controll them, is very important.

Most effective way to accomplish this purpose is by always remembering that the darkest hour is before the down of day.

Apply to your body the "Attraction Powder" after bathing, anoint your head with "Magnet Oil" each time you comb your hair, and on your clothes rub the "Has no Hanna Perfume".

Burn the "Blue and Orange Blessed Candle" for one hour whenever you find time, not more than once a day.

Do these things, my child, and let the sunshine of happiness enter your life,

SO BE IT.

TO GET RID OF EVIL SPIRITS

Oh good Mother the evil spirits seem to completely surround me. During the hours when I should be enjoying happiness and have the mental comfort which rightfully belongs to me, I find that the pressure of the evil spirits is more than I can stand.

Day and night their shadows hang over me like a dark cloud from which there is no light to be expected. Everything that I undertake with good intentions never materializes and the good fortune that was once mine has disappeared and no matter how hard I try to regain it there are always the same evil spirits blocking my progress.

Every time I feel satisfied that everything is going well and I am about to receive and accomplish that which I desire, it seems that something gets in between and I can go no farther. Finding myself in the same condition as at the beginning.

Therefore I come to you dear Mother to help me to overcome the tremendous influence that those evil spirits exercise over me, that I may be happy and contentment can once more be mine.

Oh my child you come unto me in your hour of trouble that I may bless and assist you in acquiring the happiness and good fortune that was once yours, and which have been taken away by the evil spirits created by the jealousy and envy of those who pretend to be your friends.

You will take the Get Away Powder and sprinkle it around the outside of your house at twelve o'clock midnight, you will do this for three consecutive nights. On the third night you shall begin to burn the Reversible Black Wax Candle. This you will do for thirty nights, for two hours at any hour that will be convenient for you.

In your pocket or purse, you will carry the Bat's Eye, this being the bird of the night, they will watch over you against the spirits that do the most damage during the dark hours.

After the thirty day period for burning the Reversible Black Candles have expired. then you should begin to burn your Peace Candles one at a time until you have burned three. This will strike the dreadful death blow to the haunting spirits.

My child, follow these instructions carefully and do everything that you are advised, and happiness and contentment shall be yours again.

SO BE IT.

TO CONQUER THOSE WHO HAVE MADE YOU SUFFER

Oh dear mother I come to you with tears in my eyes and weak from the pains that I have suffered through the work of my enemies.

The evil spell cast upon me by their ill intentions has caused me untold amount of mental and material torture. They have kept me awake nights when I should have been asleep. They have tired me out when I should have been resting. They have made me worry when I should have been enjoying peace, they have made me cry when I should have been smiling, they have taken away from me everything on which I have depended for happiness.

Oh dear mother I come to you to help me to reverse unto them the same evil spirit that they have cast upon me and render them helpless to again hurt me and others that may fall victim of the evil spirits and make them suffer as they have made me suffer.

Oh my child you come to me to help you in your hour of trouble. Although the spirit of revenge is not one to trifle with and is not very pleasant to handle, I will help you only as a gesture of self-defence that those who have cast upon you the spell of the evil may receive the same agony through which you have been and that it may serve as a lesson to them,

If your enemies are known to you and live in the same town, you will take the War Powder and sprinkle it in front of the house where they live so that they may step over it as they go in and out of the house.

After three days you shall take the War Water and make a cross in front of the house where your enemy lives and walk away without looking back. In front of your home you will sprinkle the Confusion Powder that it may control the evil spirits who have been hounding you and go back whence it came. Inside of your home you shall burn of the John the Conqueror Incense mixed with Helping Hand Incense and Spiritual Good Luck Incense every day.

And you will scrub your floor with water in which you have added ten drops of the Van Van Floor Wash. And you will burn one Black Wax Candle for one hour every night.

Now go forth my child and do these things according to instructions without fail and you will get your satisfaction and you will be avenged.

TO GAIN SPIRITUAL STRENGTH

The complete and reliable history of the divine revelations and the influence of wise men is found in the Scriptural monuments of the old Hebrews in the Holy Scriptures. It points out the true relation of man to the Omnipotent, it affords the most direct reference to the great truth of the Spiritual forces.

To prepare yourself for the development of the spiritualist control of the visions and interpretations of dreams, it is of paramount importance that you keep at hand at all times the Spirit Oil with which you shall anoint yourself at twelve midnight and at the same time you shall burn the white candles especially prepared for the spiritual development.

During your hours of meditation you shall have burning the Blessed Incense and Dragon Blood to install in your power to see that which is about to happen.

Professors and teachers of Spiritualism should keep by their sides the Holy Oil with which they should anoint every disciple at the beginning of each class and no less than two candles made of pure wax should be burning during such services.

The dreams will be clearer and better understood, if the seal Number 7 of the Sixth and Seventh Book of Moses, written on genuine Parchment paper with the Pure Doves Blood is worn while in bed. In this case the wearer will learn through dreams and visions what he desires.

Pour one-half teaspoon of "Dragon Blood Bath" in your bath water.

On a saucer or incense holder place 1/2 teaspoon Vesta Powder and light with a taper. Stand back so that you may see the power expelled. When the flame dies down fan the fumes over your body.

That candles were used in apostolic times in the ceremonial services of the Church is amply proven by the religious historians. The first Christians, being converts from Judaism, naturally appropriated the service of religion those symbols which were the shadow of things to come.

Among the Greeks and Romans, candles have been used as a mark of spiritual respect, and we find that under the Christian dispensation, when Bishops were received, the processions were generally led by candle bearers.

Candles are and have been for centuries, used in the administration of every spiritual sacrament. Therefore it is indispensable that every spiritual service, spiritual meditation and any devotion spiritually connected should be conducted with candle light.

SO BE IT.

THE MAN OR WOMAN IN BAD LUCK

Oh my dear Mother your child comes to you with tears in the eyes and a downcast look in the face for I have lost all that I possessed in this world. My hopes are vanishing and with no one to turn to but you, I therefore implore your help.

Restore to me the smile and happiness that once was mine. I would give part of my life for some of the luck that I used to possess. Oh Mother will you hear my prayer and help me?

My poor child I listened to your words of sorrow and gladly will I give my help that you may be lucky and happy again.

You will make a small bag of the skin of chamois. In it you will place a piece of the Lode Stone and a piece of the John the Conqueror Root and one pair of the Adam and Eve Root and a piece of the root called Devil's Shoe String. Having all of these things in the chamois bag, seal it tight that none of it may come out. This done, hold it in your left hand and with the right hand sprinkle on it five drops of the Holy Oil and at the same time read the Psalm 23 of the good book called the Bible. Place this bag in our pocket or pin it close to your skin and let it remain there allowing no one to touch it.

This bag should be anointed with the Power Oil every fifteen days. You will also use every day on your raiment and handkerchief the perfume of Astrology, better known as the Lucky Month Perfume and in your house you will burn every day the Lucky John the Conqueror Incense. Mixed with Good Luck Mystic Incense.

On the fifth day of every week, which is called Friday, recite the following prayer:

O Lord God Almighty, be Thou favorable unto us, though unworthy to lift our eyes to Heaven by reason of the multitude of our offences! O God all-merciful, who wiliest not the death of a sinner, but rather his true conversion, bestow Thy grace on us! O Lord, O God, full of compassion, aid us in this hour and grant us our desire that thy name may be blessed forever. Amen.

After doing all this my child go forth and do all that is clean and good and have no fear, but that you will receive your desired help.

SO BE IT.

THE MAN OR WOMAN WHO WISHES TO GET A JOB

0 dear Mother I come to you with a supplication which I wish you will grant me. I find myself at a loss and have no one to whom I can turn for help. Whenever I find myself where I think I am doing well the evil spirits that surround me interfere with my progress and I find myself in debt with my good friends.

At time my difficulties grow to the point that I wish that I lived no longer; therefore I beg of you dear mother to help me in this hour of need and I will be grateful to you all the days of my life.

My good child, I will hesitate not to tell you how much I sympathize with you in your dark hours, but do not give up hope, there is always a Big Almighty who watches over you twenty-four hours a day and He will not overburden you more than your frail body can stand.

It is the strong in spirit who finally attain the good wishes and the blessings of God. You shall take of the Nine Lucky Mixture and with it you will anoint your head every night at nine for nine nights and you will burn in the house the Incense of the Lucky John the Conqueror. And in your pocket or close to your skin in a chamois bag you will carry the Lucky Hand. These things should not be seen by anyone except yourself and the work should be done in complete secrecy in order to control the spirits that they will not divide their attention.

This done, my dear child, go forth and make the necessary application for your job, carrying with you the good recommendation of your former master. Do not stop on your first attempt, but keep on, and the good spirits will help you most of the way.

Stop worrying, my dear child, bring a good smile onto your face and your desires will come to pass.

SO BE IT.

THE PERSON WHO WANTS TO HOLD HIS JOB

0 Gracious Mother, I come to you with a clean heart and a clean desire, for the protection that I know only you can give me. My nerves are about to give away and fear is gradually taking possession of my soul, slowly consuming my vitality. At times I do not know whether my steps lead me forward or backward. At times my master looks upon me with scorn and disdain at other times he showers me with kindness and favors, which make me believe, and I feel that the evil spirits are working against me, and this job that I now have and which I would like to keep is gently slipping from under me.

Now dear mother I again beg you to help me keep my position around which I have built my hopes.

My dear child as you have well stated in your faithful request the good and evil spirits are working for you and against you. You have neglected to do the things which you should have done in harmony with the good spirits and destruction of the evil ones, but if you will bow to my command, I will help you to eliminate the spirit of gloom that constantly hovers over your head, leaving you in an uncertain state of mind.

You will take the hone of the black cat and the heart of the Swallow and you will place them in a small bag made of the skin of the chamois. This bag you will pin on your raiment touching your skin and every week you shall anoint it with five drops of the Fast Luck Drops and every day you shall use freely of the God's Water which you find plentiful in your home faucet in the form of a bath in which you will pour nine drops of the Oil of Rosemary for the purpose of cleansing your body that the obnoxious odor will disappear and nothing but Fresh sweet scent will remain. You shall never let frowns appear on your face as it tends to draw the spirit of evils making it more difficult for the good spirits to do their work.

At bed time you will repeat the following prayers:

O great and living God, who hast created man to enjoy felicity in this life who has adopted all things for his necessity and didst declare that everything should be made subject to his will. Be favorable to this, my prayer, and permit not the evil spirits to be in possession of my body and soul. Grant me 0 Great God, the power to dispose of them through your help and I will forever remain thy faithful and obedient servant.

Amen.

SO BE IT.

HOW TO IMPROVE YOUR CONDITION

My child, if things do not seem to move in the direction you desire after many efforts to advance without result, no doubt there is a cross force impeding your progress. This impediment can be best removed by getting at the root of the condition. You may suspect some one holding you back intentionally or you may suspect some other psychic phenomena.

At any event, take care of yourself. Light a "Double Action Candle" for one hour every day.

Pour ten drops of "Special Oil No. 20" in the water in which you bathe. After the bath, powder your chest with "Uncrossing Powder", and anoint your garment and head with a few drops of "Nine Lucky Mixture".

Burn in your house once each day the "Spiritualist Good Luck Incense". Go your way with luck and peace.

SO BE IT.

ADVICE TO SPIRITUALISTS AND MEDIUMS

My Friends, I know most of you have the desires to help and to comfort those that come before you with supplications, tears in their eyes, painful heart, with trouble that mounts from day to day, with no one to turn to but you, but sometimes you are also burdened with your own troubles in addition to the unfortunate afflictions of others.

It is not an easy path. It is absolutely necessary that you be in complete control of all your faculties. If you aim to help, according to the spiritual law, you must first be strong spiritually in order that you may absorb the power so essential in the process of helping others. In order to help yourself, and acquire the power to help others, follow these instructions:

On arising in the morning the first thing to do is to anoint your head with "Power Oil", light two blessed candles, white in color, and meditate for fifteen minutes. In your main room or consultation room a seven day candle should always be burning. Be sure it is blessed. Dress your home with "Peace Water" at least once a week and in your bath water pour five drops of "Master Oil". Sprinkle "Jinx Removing Salt" on the outside of your house.

Strength will be yours.

SO BE IT.

PROSPERITY

My child, the Law of the Spirit is co-create. The Law of the Creator is concrete. The Law of Mankind is often questionable.

Prosperity is here for all to attain if approached the proper and ethical way. Mortality and conscience. Fair play and decency. Consideration, respect, altruism, 'good humor, faith, goodness, benevolence and sacrifice.

Prosperity can be yours, but it must be bought with fortitude and tenacity. Patience is also very important in the strenuous trek to prosperity.

Do the following things and help yourself on the way up.

Burn for one hour each day the "Prosperity Candle" anointed with "King Solomon Oil" Burn in your house a mixture of "Good Luck Incense" and "Helping Hand Incense" Spray your house with "Divine Spray" and apply the "Drawing Powder" to your neck and chest daily.

Stay out of too much debt. Do not be a slave. Protect your income. Good luck.

SO BE IT.

HOW TO INFLUENCE PEOPLE

My dear child, you come to me because you seek help. You have been devoid of the power to influence those you came in contact with.

It is written, my child, that you shall follow these instructions to accomplish your desire.

It is very important that your body be clean at all times as well as your raiment.

Pour ten drops of the oil called "Special Oil No. 20" in your bath water, after bathing apply to your body the "Controlling Powder" and rub in your hands and clothing the "Bend Over Drops". Burn in your house a combination of "Mixture of John the Conqueror Incense" and "Helping Hand Incense" every day.

Use the Master Oil as a perfume every day.

Do these things with faith and ask God to help you.

SO BE IT.

HOW TO ATTRACT ATTENTION

My friend, sometimes it seems as though everything is against us and whatever we attempt to do turns up in the opposite direction. We find it very difficult to find the way to straighten things out. When we almost reach our goal or our desire something always happens to upset our progress and things we were reaching for disappear into nothing, leaving us in a state of want and despair.

Here, my child, take it with more calm and faith and fill your heart with hope.

Burn the "Triple Action Candle" every day anointed with "Altar Oil" for one hour.

Anoint your head with "High Conquering Oil", apply "Drawing powder" to your body every day, and pour one half teaspoonful of the "Dragon Blood Bath" in your bath water.

Use the "Nine Lucky Mixture" as regular perfume. God bless you.

SO BE IT.

THE BEST GAMBLING HAND

(Toby)

You will take the Nutmeg of India. in it you will drill a hole in which you will pour the Pure Mercury and seal it with pure wax. After this take a piece of chamois 3% in. in length by 31/2 in. in width and make it into a small bag. In this bag you will put a piece of Highly magnetic Lode Stone, a Black Cat Bone, the heart of a Swallow, the John the Conqueror Root, Devil Shoe String and the Five Finger Grass, then on top of all of this you will place the prepared nutmeg of India. This done seal the bag by sewing it all the way around so that none of these articles may fall out. And on the outside of this bag you shall sprinkle three drops of Jockey Club Perfume once every week. Keep this bag on your person at all times and allow no one to touch it.

INSTRUCTION FOR DRESSING HOMES, PLACES BUSI-
NESS AND CHURCHES

Place on the floor of each room a saucer or small tin can almost filled with water and in each saucer pour ten drops of Oil of Rosemary and let them remain there until they are through with the Dressing. In each room you will light one DEVOTIONAL CANDLE and let them remain lighted until they have burned out by themselves. Then you will take a bottle of War Water and empty it in a basin or pail and add two quarts of Hot Water and mix well. With your hand, you will sprinkle of this mixture every corner in every room. While doing this you will murmur in a low voice the following words:

EZEKIEL, ISRAELIS, MAY THE BLESSINGS OF' GOD ENTER HERE. AMEN

After every room in the house has been sprinkled, you will use the remaining water in the pail or basin and with it you shall make a cross outdoors in the rear of your house, business place or church. If the place to be dressed is upstairs, you shall throw this water out doors through any rear window. This done, you shall proceed by placing some John the Conqueror Incense in the incense burner or small saucer and carry it through every room to be dressed. Returning to the room from which you started, and there you shall kneel in front of the burning devotional candles and repeat the following prayer.

Almighty God, we beseech thee mercifully to incline thine ears to us who have now made our prayers and supplications unto thee; and grant that those things which we have faithfully asked according to thy will, may effectually be obtained to the relief of our necessity, and to the setting forth of thy glory.

Rise from there and take the NINE LUCKY MIXTURE and sprinkle three drops in every corner of every room that luck may come and bad forces may leave. After this read the 91st Psalm which you will find in your Bible. When you have finished reading this Psalm you will gather all of the dishes that contained the Oil of Rosemary and Water, and pour into a bottle so that it will be saved to be used by sprinkling a few drops of it in the front part of your house until it is all consumed. After this, kneel again before the first candle that you have lighted and read the twenty-first psalm out of your good book, the Bible. Be very careful to let the Devotional Candles burn out before moving them away. When you have done all of these things, my dear child, only the divine blessing must be expected for darkness will turn to sunshine, and sadness to gladness, and woe to happiness. May God he with you.-Amen.

THE NOVENA

This ancient religious custom has been handed down from generation to generation even before the coming of Christ and was practiced by the ancient Hebrews and is not practiced by the Christians of all denominations.

It is also practiced by the Chinese in different form, by the Brahmins and was handed down by the Egyptians.

It consists of burning nine candles on nine different days or nights and burning one at a time.

The Egyptian custom was that under each candle the wish that is asked for shall be written on pure parchment paper or papyrus, or in case you wish to influence some particular person, the name of that person is written on the parchment paper and put under each candle as it is burned, in such a manner that the wax shall fall on the paper and cover it as it burns.

Also a prayer is said before each candle as it burned and when it is first lighted this prayer most ask what the person wants and must be prayed for earnestly and with fervor and piety. Some persons practice this with a photograph of the person they wish to influence under the candle instead of the parchment with the name on it, but the old practice is always with the parchment under it. It is also very important that the candles will not blow out after once it is lit, for if the candles blow out it is a sign of ill omen and the novena should begin all over again as if you had started a new one.

It has been asked over and over again what is a novena, what does it mean, what is its objective. The answer, that it is a Latin word as now used, and its meaning is a new beginning, in other words, you leave all the old behind and begin a new life just as if you were born again, the sense being akin to the resurrection and it leaves your sins behind you, giving a new aspect and is a new look into your life, without being burdened by your old sins and your old mistakes.

So it is that a lady can ask in a novena that her husband shall come back to her and allow all of his old loves to die in him and only remember that he will begin life all over again with her, and it is possible that it shall be all over again with her, and it is possible that it shall be granted to her. So a man ask that all of his old sins, mistakes and even his debts of honor shall be forgiven him and make a novena on that, and he shall have the right to begin all over again, in fact make a new start, provided of course that he really takes his lesson to heart, and that he shall do better in the future.

So a boy can ask for understanding in his studies and his duties so that he can become a success in his chosen employment and it may be given to him, and all his old mistakes will be left behind him and all the old misgivings and uncertainties will leave him and so make him a grand success in his chosen employment, where otherwise he might not have been able to make a living for himself before. And so may things which you wish to forget, the things which you may wish that other to forgive and which you wish to forgive to others are wiped from the slate of your memory and are forgotten and left behind all for your benefit and peace of mind so that you can get a better chance to live by the aid of the novena.

OUTSTANDING SIGNIFICANCE OF CANDLES

Prosperity .... Red or Green
Love.. Pink or Red
Peace .... White
Attraction .... Yellow
Dispelling (blessed) .... Black
Novena .... Nine Days Candle
Special Devotion or Supplication......... Nine Devotional Candles
Revenge.. Double Action Reversible Black

Prayer Meetings, Circles, Classes, etc., use the Seven Candles of the Spectrum consisting of Pink, Red, Blue, Yellow, White, Orange, and Purple. In small groups two White Candles will be sufficient.

Work .... Purple
Vibration .... White and Pink
For Reading or Special Spiritual Messages .... Red and White
Protection .... Reversible Double Action
Holidays .... White or Wax
Concentration .... Purple and White
Success .... Triple Action
Special Favors .... Brown
Friendship .... Blue
Happiness .... Blue and Orange
Influence .... Brown and Pink
To Pray for the Sick .... White

If you were born in	January	born	Red and Gold
" " "	February	"	Yellow and Blue
" " "	March	"	Blue and Green
" " "	April	"	Pink and Orange
" " "	May	"	Blue and Gold
" " "	June	"	Red and Blue
" " "	July	"	Red and Green
" " "	August	"	Pink and Orange
" " "	September	"	Pink and Gold
" " "	October	"	Pink and Gold
" " "	November	"	Yellow and Blue
" " "	December	"	Red and Orange

DEVOTION

Candles have been placed in this world to provide the faithful means of showing their devotion in a tangible manner.

It is recommended to those lighting candles that while doing so they make use of the following prayer:

May this offering, I pray Thee, O Lord, both loose the bonds of my sins, and win for the gift of thy Blessed mercy

You have the power to create whatsoever you will pertaining to human life; you have the power to determine what you shall create and when and where you wish to create it, and it also means that you have the power to create what you want N-O-W.

Never, as long as you live, can you rid your life of disagreeable people, as long as you have the qualities of consciousness which attract them. Eliminate the destructive states of thought and you will no longer have your life made miserable by offensive, obnoxious and disgusting persons who seemingly live to annoy you and who always misunderstood you.

So you can see how important it is never to express in thought, word or deed, any of the destructive emotions, and to think only thoughts which express the emotions of love, truth, faith, gratitude and praise toward every condition, every circumstance and every person in your life.

It is the common lot of all to make enemies. The successful man or woman becomes so by virtue of transmitting each enemy into a friend; and mediocre men or women remain so because they not only make enemies, but keep them as such.

Get the habit of making one new friend each day and putting forth a sincere effort to bind an old one closer to you. However, you cannot do this by gossip, criticism, or passing derogatory remarks about anyone.

SIGNIFICANCE OF THE CARDS

The following definitions are based upon one of the oldest authorities dealing with the subject, and have been amplified by some of the more modern meanings in vogue:

SPADES

Ace.-It may concern love affairs, or convey a warning that troubles await the inquirer through bad speculations or ill-chosen friends.

King.-A dark man. Ambitious and successful in the higher walks of life.

Queen-A widow, of malicious and unscrupulous nature, fond of scandal and open to bribes.

Jack.-A well-meaning, inert person, unready in action though kindly in thought.

Ten.-An evil omen; grief or imprisonment. Has power to detract from the good signified by cards near it.

Nine.-An ill-fated card, meaning sickness, losses, troubles, end family dissensions.

Eight.-A warning with regard to any enterprise in hand. This card close to the inquirer means evil; also opposition from friends.

Seven.-Sorrow caused by the loss of a dear friend.

Six.-Hard work brings wealth and rest after toil.

Five.-Bad temper and a tendency to interfere in the inquirer, but happiness to be found in the chosen wife or husband.

Four. Illness and the need for great attention to business.

Three.-A marriage that will be marred by the inconstancy of the inquirer's wife or husband; or a journey.

Deuce.-A removal, or possibly death.

In connection with the foregoing detailed explanation of the meanings of each card in an ordinary pack, we append a short table which may be studied either separately or with the preceding definitions. It gives at a glance certain broad outlines, which may be of use to one who wishes to acquire the art of reading a card directly it is placed before the eye:

HEARTS

Ace.-An important card, whose meaning is affected by its environment. Among hearts it implies love, friendship, and affection, with diamonds, money and news of distant friends, spades, disagreements, misunderstandings, contention, or misfortune; individually, it stands for the house.

King.--A good hearted man, with strong affections, emotional, and given to rash judgments, possessing more zeal than discretion.

Queen.--A fair woman, loving and lovable, domesticated, prudent, and faithful,

Jack.---Not endowed with any sex. Sometimes taken as Cupid; also as the best friend of the inquirer, or as a fair person's thoughts. The cards on either side of the knave are indicative of the good or bad nature of its intentions.

Ten.-A sign of good fortune. It implies a good heart, happiness, and the prospect of a large family. It contends had cards and confirms god ones in its vicinity.

Nine.-The wish card. It is the sign of riches, and of high social position accompanied by influence and esteem. It may be affected by the neighborhood of bad cards.

Eight.-The pleasures of the table, convivial society. Another meaning implies love and marriage.

Seven.-A faithless, inconsistent friend who may prove an enemy.

Six.-A confiding nature, liberal, open-handed, and an easy prey for swindlers; courtship and a possible proposal.

Five,-Causeless jealousy in a person of weak, unsettled character.

Four.-One who has remained single till middle life being too hard to please.

Three.-A warning card as to the possible results of the inquirer's own want of prudence and tact.

Deuce.-Prosperity and success in a measure dependent on the surrounding cards; endearments and wedding bells.

DIAMONDS

Ace.-A ring or paper money.

King.-A fair man, with violent temper and vindictive, obstinate turn of mind.

Queen.-A fair woman, given to flirtation, fond of society and admiration.

Jack.-A near relative who puts his own interests first, is self-opinionated, easily offended, and not always quite straight. It may mean a fair person's thoughts.

Ten. - Plenty of money, a husband or wife from the country, and several children.

Nine.-This card is influenced by the one accompanying it; if the latter be a court card, the person referred to will have his capacities discounted by a restless, wandering disposition. It may imply a surprise connected with money, or if in conjunction with the eight of spades it signifies crossed swords.

Eight.-A marriage late in life, which will probably be somewhat checkered.

Seven.-This card has various meanings. It enjoins the need for careful action. It may imply a decrease of prosperity. Another reading connects it with uncharitable tongues.

Six.-An early marriage and speedy widowhood. A warning with regard to second marriage is also included.

Five.-To young married people this portends good children. In a general way it means unexpected news, or success in business enterprises.

Four.-Breach of confidence. Troubles caused by inconstant friends, vexatious and disagreeable.

Deuce.-An unsatisfactory love affair, awakening opposition from relatives or friends.

G·D THIE RS

CLUBS

Ace.-Wealth, a peaceful home, industry, and general prosperity.

King.-A dark man of upright, high-minded nature, calculated to make an excellent husband, faithful and true in his affections.

Queen.-A dark woman, with a trustful, affectionate disposition with great charm for the opposite sex, and unsuceptible to male attractions.

Jack.-A generous, trusty friend, who will take trouble on behalf of the inquirer. It may also mean a dark man's thoughts.

Ten.-Riches suddenly acquired, probably through the death of a relation or friend.

Nine.-Friction through opposition to the wishes of friends

Eight.-Love of money, and a passion for speculating.

Seven.-Great happiness and good fortune. If troubles come they will be caused by one of the opposite sex to the inquirer.

Six.-Success in business, both for self and children.

Five.-An advantageous marriage.

Four.-A warning against falsehood and double-dealing.

Three.-Two or possibly three marriages with money.

Deuce.-There is needed to avert disappointment and to avoid opposition.

CAPRICORN

(THE GOAT)

IF YOU WERE BORN BETWEEN DECEMBER 22 AND JANUARY 20

The people of Capricorn are naturally inclined to study and deep thinking, and many of the deep thinkers, natural orators and teachers of the world are to be found in this sign. Those of this sign who are fairly well educated have a burning and persistent thirst for more education and knowledge, and will never rest as long as their intellectual attainments are not of the highest.

These people resent interferences of others who will tell them how to run their affairs, and they seldom meddle with the affairs of other people. They understand that the secret to success is to attend strictly to their own business. It is much better for Capricorn people to be in business for themselves. They work hard and with great pleasure for themselves, but they are miserable and restless when in the employ of others.

At times they are brilliant and full of life. At times they become depressed, melancholy, and blue, and at such times they seek to be alone. They are magnetic and hypnotic, and naturally attract people. They should get a good business education and learn to be self-maintaining and self-reliant. This suggestion applies to both sexes.

Capricorn people are often indiscreet and eccentric in their charities and investments. At times they will give with a lavish hand and at other times they will not give at all, and this all depends on the mood they are in. Some of them live too much in the external, and are very proud, arrogant, and dictatorial. They are naturally. Independent and self-reliant, and are lovers of harmony and beauty. At times they are very high-spirited and all the world looks bright to them, and at other times they are depressed and gloomy and seek to be alone.

Capricorn people are very magnetic and draw people to them without any effort, which is due to a magnetic law. They are very proud and abhor all flattery. They are cool and calm, as are most people in earth sings, and are not impulsive or demonstrative. They love order, and are easily confused when working under other people who have no system, and often become stubborn and angry. They are quick to know their friends, and can discriminate between flattery and sincerity. It is sometimes very hard to get them to look beyond the external life, but when they once become awakened, control the animal nature and material tendencies, and learn the spiritual truths, they become very enthusiastic and faithful religious workers.

The women of this sign are usually very attractive, and are among the most devoted wives and housekeepers. They are very orderly and systematic, and must be permitted to have their own way about the household. They are clean, neat, and proud, and possess rare ability in the arrangement and management of the home. These women do not display their affections and often appear to be dignified and cold. But they are very constant in their love, even to the extent of being jealous of those they love. Many of them feel that the domestic world is too small, and seek employment in the business world.

The ruling planet of this sign is Saturn. The Lucky gem is the Garnet and Monday is the Lucky day.

Lucky Blessed Candles Red and Old Gold.

69.32.3 ---- 13.44.7 ---- 732.417.576

AQUARIUS

(THE WATER BEARER)

IF YOU WERE BORN BETWEEN JANUARY 20 AND FEBRUARY 19

Aquarius people are among the strongest and the weakest in the world. They can rise to the highest heights or be utter failures. To what extent they may go lies within themselves, for they can make themselves what they wish. They are naturally endowed with great possibilities, and it is entirely their own fault if they don't succeed.

One great fault with Aquarius people is that they are not sufficiently self-reliant. They will earnestly seek advice from others, to which they pay not the slightest attention. They will ask questions and forget the answers. They can always remember what they see, but forget what they hear. At times they are happy and the world looks bright and cheerful, and at other times they are much depressed.

These people possess unusual powers, but often neglect using them, and for those who have become awakened and are using their talents, their reward is very great. Some of the greatest spiritual healers that we have are horn under this sign, and every Aquarius person is a natural healer, but very few of them are aware of it. These people should realize that they really can amount to something, and should try to improve their opportunities and not sit about deploring their misfortune or inability to succeed.

Aquarius people often talk too much about their affairs to other people, and should be careful as to what other people think about their actions. They must learn to have the utmost confidence in their ability to succeed in any undertaking, and press forward and onward until they have reached their goal. Aquarius people are not usually deceived, and are the best judges of character.

Aquarius people have the faculty of learning things without much study. They seem to attract and observe information from every source. They seldom memorize anything, and it is not necessary for them to do so. As a rule they are very pleasing and agreeable, with dignity on all occasions. They are quiet, calm, and peaceful people, with excellent control of their passions, seldom are ill-tempered, and make many friends. They spend their entire lives in the service of others.

It is usually the women of this sign who carry the news from one neighbor to another and spread the gossip. As long as people exercise and disturb themselves about the faults of others they keep themselves excited and in a weakened condition. These people must learn to seek for good in all things and never look on the bad side of life.

Aquarius people should learn to depend upon no one but themselves, be independent and self-reliant, ask favors of no one, stand on their own feet, and not lean on anyone. They should learn to use their own brains. Advice as a rule is worth just what you pay for it.

The women of this sign have easy, graceful manners, and are very loyal to their mates. They are quite talkative. They must learn to bridle their tongues, and always remember that silence is golden.

The ruling stars of this sign are Uranus, symbol of friendship, and Saturn (Fate and Destiny). The Lucky gem is the Amethyst and Friday is the Lucky day.

Lucky Blessed Candles Yellow and Blue.

12.37.14 ---- 59.28.12   ---- 918.429.962

PISCES

(THE FISHES)
IF YOU WERE BARN BETWEEN FEBRUARY 19 AND MARCH 21

Pisces people are natural lovers, and their love is generally high and pure, and often goes out to the world in general. They are generally honest, and seldom look for dishonesty or deceit in others. They are noble, generous, and wish to help all who are in need, and are often deceived through having too much faith in human nature. They are sometimes deceived by their nearest friends. They are very loyal to their friends, can seldom see a flaw in them, and will stay by them through thick and thin.

Cultured and educated people of this sign readily discern the picturesque in everything. Being a psychic sign, they can sense the feelings of others, and they attract people to them. Thy often give away all they possess to help others, and then worry because they cannot help more. This is the power and force of their great love.

They would do well to use more common sense and judgment, and not waste all their forces for others. They are very charming and lovable people, and are often found in positions of trust and great responsibility.

Few egotists are found in this sign. They have little or nothing to say about their abilities, and in many cases underestimate themselves; and because of their lack of self-esteem they are often embarrassed and it makes them feel that all the world is against them. With their beautiful nature and the great powers they possess they should set about at once to overcome this feeling.

Many Pisces people are inclined to be careless, and will lose and misplace articles. The women are careless housekeepers, which is mostly due to nervous fear. They must learn the value of courage and confidence and perseverance before they can hope to rise to any great height.

When they are living on the lower plane of life or in a bad mental state of mind, advice to them is useless, and they will listen to no one. The more they are talked to the more obstinate they become. They talk too much and ask all kinds of unreasonable questions, and make themselves disagreeable to all with whom they come in contact. They often break into conversation with some silly remark, clearly indicating that they were not paying the slightest attention to what was being said.

The women of Pisces are kind-hearted and generous, and after they have overcome their desire to chance and travel they become devoted wives and mothers. They often become worried, despondent, and melancholy over trifles that never come to pass. They should overcome all worry and anxiety, and dwell more in the present and less in the future. Many women of this sign are very pretty, have beautiful form, soft features, and beautiful eyes. The ruling planets of the Pisces sign are Neptune and Jupiter. The lucky gem is the Bloodstone and Wednesday is the Lucky Day.

Lucky Blessed Candles Blue and Green.
29.73.48 ---- 63.15-26 ---- 167.368.218

ARIES

(THE RAM)
IF YOU WERE BORN BETWEEN MARCH 21 MID APRIL 20

People of this sign know no fear or opposition, and swing through life overriding all obstacles. These people are unequalled in earnestness and determination, and many of the world's greatest leaders were born in this sign. They are natural commanders, and usually dominate all about them. They like to lay out their own work and do it in their own way, and should never be interfered with, as interference of others often causes them to fly into a rage and to abandon their undertakings. They are natural leaders, and feel that they should he at the head of affairs. They have a keen sense of justice and when in position of authority are seldom, if ever, one-sided, and with all their natural desire to rule and command are generous, gentle, noble and kind; very magnetic and progressive.

All Aries people have a fiery temper, despite being commanded, and cannot work well under other people, as they are natural leaders and feel that they should he at the head of affairs. They are very independent, and have high and lofty ideas, and few things come up to their expectations. These people are original in thought and ideas, are ambitious, energetic, and reliable, and quite capable of rising to great heights in the world.

They can often sense the feelings of others without exchanging a single word. As a rule they are honest and square and will die fighting for a principle. They stay by their friends to the last and the more people criticize them the better they like them. They love to entertain their friends and are lovers of dancing and music, always dressed well, and often appear to be wealthier than they really are, which may be accounted for by their commanding appearance.

Aries people are very good-natured and always ready to help those in distress. They are interested in politics, but are not the best of politicians on account of their fiery temper. They enter every battle to win, and never acknowledge defeat. But if they should lose disappointment is very great.

It is hard to deceive an Aries person, once he has recognized his power of intuition. When they have developed the gifts of spirit, they will then grasp all, and they should press onward and open their soul to the eternal, and will then realize the great peace, happiness and prosperity that belting to them.

Aries women in many ways are most charming. They are very handsome and efficient, and would have the most beautiful temperament if it were not for their desire to rule and lead the parade, and a quick temper and jealousy, which are the great stumbling blocks in their way. They are often extravagant to their dress, fond of nice clothes as long as they are new. If they knew the great possibilities before them, they would learn self-control, and would school the mind to be the master. Without this no true peace can come to them. Aries sign is ruled by the energetic planet Mars, the Lucky gem is Diamond. Thursday is the Lucky day.

Lucky Blessed Candles Pink and Orange.
8.41.62 ---- 26.71.38 ---- 183.274.385

TAURUS

(THE BULL)

IF YOU WERE BORN BETWEEN APRIL 20 AND MAY 21

People born under this sign are remarkable in many respects. They are kind, gentle, often very generous, and overload themselves with the burdens of others. They are continually thinking about helping others, and often become miserable because they cannot help more than they do. Money to them is of no value only for the good it will do, and because of a generous impulse they are often imposed upon by a tale of woe.

Taurus people have wonderful personalities. They are bright, witty, fond of dancing and music, and with their sympathetic, winning manner, they adapt themselves to all classes of society. They are magnetic and very well liked and take very much pleasure in the friendships they form. They are close-mouthed, seldom talkative, but their mental powers lie very deep, and people soon learn to rely upon their advice and encouragement. Not having an abundance of reasoning ability, they are often guided by intuition.

These people are very much set in their ways, and once their minds are made up arguments and persuasions are useless. They will carry out their ideas regardless of consequences.

The animal nature is so strongly marked in Taurus people from birth that they have certain tendencies toward debasing habits and modes of life which may be destroyed with the practice of self-control. Undeveloped Taurus people are the most unreasonable on earth. They demand their own way in the pursuit of pleasures, and opposition or resistance causes them to fly into an outburst of anger or violence. They rave and rant and wreak their anger on whatever may stand in their path. They are dangerous to live with and the only thing to do is to get out of their way until the violence has spent itself and reason has returned. They are often money hungry, and would like the whole world for themselves. They love their own ease, pleasure and comfort. The lot of a wife with such a person is apt to be filled with sadness and misery, for they insist upon ruling absolutely in the home. With self-control all the evil passions and tendencies, with their terrible consequences, will be overcome, and the fine character of this sign will shine forth in all its beauty.

The women of this sign must be exceedingly careful not to be led astray by sympathy or flattery. Taurus people have the strongest passions of the twelve signs, and the Taurus maiden is overly lavish in her affection, with the result that a hasty marriage is often made early in life, which usually proves a failure. These women have all the beauty of Venus, and are surrounded with wonderful planetary and solar influences and open to all the new discoveries of progress.

They can command all the powers of the universe if they would only raise to the higher plane of life and control their animal nature. Until this is done much trouble comes to them and they are disliked by everyone about them. The ruling planet of the

Taurus sign is Venus. Lucky gem is the Emerald. Lucky day is Tuesday. Lucky Blessed Candles Blue and Old Gold.

26.34.47 ---- 39-56.78 ---- 917.826.735

GEMINI

(THE TWINS)
IF YOU WERE BORN BETWEEN MAY 21 AND JUNE 22

People born under this sign have remarkable intellects, and are gifted in anything that calls for a quick, receptive mind. They are extremely affectionate and generous; courteous, considerate, kind and gentle to all. They are very magnetic and lovable and have many friends.

A true Gemini person is a remarkable individual and some of the most wonderful people in the world were born in this sign. Gemini people must learn to control their double nature. They are happy and unhappy at the same time. They are in love and they are not in love. They want to travel and they want to stay at home. When they are married they want to be single, and when they are single they want to be married. They want to be rich and they want to be poor. In short, they are of a restless disposition and are forever changing from one place to another. They often make a lot of money, but they do not save it.

Their family pride is great, and they are fond of tracing back into family history. They are proud of birth. Little selfishness or meanness is found among these people. In fact, they are often too generous for their own good. Gemini people seldom worry about the future, and often meet with extreme poverty before they learn the value of money; and then they will change over-night and become the most successful people in the world, and being extremely generous they often help, to their sorrow, many whom they believe to be friends. They have a quick, receptive mind and can see both sides of any proposition, but as a rule they are not a success as wage earners. They belong in business for themselves, although as traveling salesmen or in some line of transportation where there is a continuous change through travel and meeting new people they will remain a long time with one corporation.

They are lovers of books and read many stories, and perhaps cover a far wider range in their studies than any other people in the world. They are brilliant in conversation and can talk intelligently on almost any subject. They are often masters of many languages.

With Gemini people, most marriages take place on impulse. There are two kinds of love, one a passionate love that soon fades and dies, and the other a true affectionate love that vibrates between two harmonious signs of the Zodiac-and these people should ever strive to associate with quiet, calm, thoughtful people. They are most apt to find harmony with those born in Aquarius, Sagittarius, and Virgo, and children of such union are usually physically and mentally strong.

Gemini being an air sign, they are a fast, but steadfast and sure type of people, and very determined. This will modify and bring more of a steadfast quality to the restless and changeable disposition of the Gemini subject.

Gemini sign is ruled by the planet Mercury. Lucky day is Saturday.

Lucky Blessed Candles Red and Blue.
38.56.23 ---- 9.74.48 ---- 187.476.359

CANCER

(THE CRAB)
IF YOU WERE BORN BETWEEN JUNE 22 AND JULY 23

The moon being the ruling planet of the Cancer sign, it gives them a very changeable nature. They are extremely sensitive and often go through life without being understood, and sometimes do not understand themselves.

Cancer people are naturally endowed with strong determination, intuition and purpose, and if they will persistently push forward and not give up they are sure to reach success. Arguments have not much effect with these people. Their feelings are too easily hurt, and they often abandon big undertakings because of slights or criticism. They are at times very strong and at other times very weak. They go to extremes which cause their friends to marvel.

Education and culture to Cancer people is of untold advantage. They like changes of scene and occupation, and are apt to waste a lot of time in learning new things. These tendencies are good when not carried to extreme. Cancer people are tender-hearted and sympathetic, and often very generous. Their interest in public welfare is very strong at times, and in some cases when they cannot lend a helping hand they become very gloomy.

Cancer people, when not developed, often talk too much, especially the women, who will seldom keep a secret. They talk too much about themselves and the great things they have done. In time this grows to be a disease, and it makes them considered by all utterly unreliable, and then they have a hard time to get along in the world.

During the day these people are very happy, while at night they become blue and depressed and unhappy, and at this time the world does not look very bright, and they are nervous and restless. It is then that they should seek some quiet spot and meditate on the higher things of life. This will bring calm and repose, and change the darkest and gloomiest nights to brightness.

Cancer women are among the most attractive, as they have most charming personalities. Many beautiful women come out of this sign. They are neat, and like to be looked up to.

These women are fickle, changeable and hard to understand, and often display their changeable nature in rearranging the furniture in the home. They are lovers of children and pets, and as this sign rules over the breast they have a natural tendency to mother. However, they should not marry young in life, but should wait until they become more settled, for as a rule in early life they are not satisfied with any one thing for any length of time, and often discard a friend without the slightest reason.

Cancer people are natural horn merchants and have inventive ability. They are often very successful manufacturers, and are well adapted for active trade and business. They do not like to be hampered or restricted in any way. They are fond of the stock market and gambling, and have a natural tendency toward the beautiful and artistic.

Some excellent musicians, artists, and professional men are produced by this sign, also lawyers and public speakers.

The fruitful moon is Cancer's ruling planet, Ruby the Lucky gem and Tuesday the Lucky day.

Lucky Blessed Candles Red and Green.

14.43.62 ---- 27.39.58 ---- 638.917.425

LEO

(THE LION)
IF YOU WERE BORN BETWEEN JULY 23 AND AUGUST 23

Leo people, owing to their natural goodness, create a happy future. When the true individuality of this sign holds full sway then they have high ideals, loyalty, pure and abundant love, and will give up all comfort to care for and nurse the sick. They are always ready to lend a helping hand. They never forget a favor, and never forget an injury.

These people are fearless and courageous, and often carry their plans to extremes regardless of consequence, but they have the power of mind to override all difficulties. They have courage and determination that commands the highest respect and admiration. These people have a great love for children, and as to the management of their own are exceedingly wise, as they will not yield to the dictation of others.

They are generally square and honest in all business dealings, and seldom, if ever forsake a friend. The undeveloped Leo has many faults, but they can all be cured by following the teachings of astrology, and it is of utmost importance that Leo people strengthen their weak points, as their possibilities are great. Those living on the lower plane are often exceedingly impatient, hot-headed, easily angered, fiery and passionate, and sometimes cunning and tricky, and they are often chronic borrowers. Much of their misery is brought on through their strong affection and passion for the opposite sex.

Leo people often form their likes and dislikes at a glance and in most cases they are right. However, it is best for them not to jump to conclusions so quickly, as they will sometimes make mistakes that will cause them sorrow, loss, and pain. When their faults are overcome and they have risen to a higher plane and wish to live a useful life, there are no better or more helpful people in all the signs, and no more magnetic or lovable people in the world when the higher nature rules. It is then that these people are very successful-when they have controlled their appetites and passions. Leo people should not allow themselves to become despondent or blue, for such a state of mind is very dangerous and may bring on serious illness.

After Leo people have met great trouble, adversity, loss, and sickness, it is then that they will wake up and realize their faults and begin to think of higher and better things; and there is no limit to the great things in store for them when they once realize their higher nature.

The selfishness of this sign must he entirely killed, and they should always have regard For the happiness of others, for only woe, misery, unhappiness, and discontent can come to a selfish person.

Some of the gayest, most emotional, loving women in all the world are found in Leo. There is a glow of sunshine that seems to linger about them.

The ruling planet of Leo is the Sun, Sardonyx is the Lucky gem and Monday the Lucky day.

Lucky Blessed Candles Pink and Orange.
30.43.56 ---- 13.11.18 ---- 618.323.746

VIRGO

(THE VIRGIN)
IF YOU WERE BORN BETWEEN AUGUST 23 AND SEPTEMBER 23

Virgo people possess a great deal of magnetism, and among them are often found magnetic healers. They are very generous and loyal, They usually lake great interest in the love affairs of their acquaintances and friends, and the women of Virgo have a propensity for making matches and selecting companions for their children, and they take the same interest in breaking them.

Virgo people are very affectionate and devoted to their families. While lacking somewhat in courage and application at times they aspire to become good and great people, and among those of high intellect and culture there is no lack of continuity. They can overcome all obstacles with grace and ease, and are usually actively occupied in some elevating pursuit. The intellectually developed Virgo person fully realizes that lost moments and lost opportunities are sunken pearls.

The possibilities of Virgo people are very great when they once recognize that there is perfect unity in the universe and that what often appears to be wrong is right, that man and the world are evolving and some good is found in all bad. The faults in undeveloped Virgo people are numerous but they will seldom acknowledge or recognize their own faults, although they are continually and persistently seeing the faults in others.

It appears at times that Virgo people are so busy with the affairs of others that they have not a moment to examine themselves. One of the great faults of many Virgo people is their determination to rule and domineer all other people about them. They interfere with other people's affairs, are extremely critical and always criticizing the faults of others, and this tendency makes them disagreeable and unpopular. The greatest people in all history have been those who have attended to their own affairs. Virgo people often have a weakness for wealth and positions of authority. They are full of false pride and ambition, and many imitators are to be found among them. Interfering with the affairs of others and unduly criticizing others is only a lack common sense. God never intended us to judge our fellow beings harshly or to interfere with their sacred rights. It must be remembered that every individual was intended to have the right to freedom of thought.

Most of the lower type of Virgo people have a great weakness for appearing well, and feel that the good things of life should be theirs. As a result, they often sacrifice honor and character to keep up appearances or to get before the public. This is especially true of the women, who will resort to deception and exaggeration, and frequently get hopelessly into debt in consequence. Virgo people as a rule are very healthy, hut they imagine they have all sorts of ills and are apt to keep continually experimenting with drugs, medicines, and physicians. The points outlined here are the ways of Virgo people and it rests entirely with them to secure all joy, peace, happiness and prosperity or go through life filled with misery, sadness and unhappiness.

Many beautiful and charming women come out of this sign, and love and purity seem to linger about them, they love companions and are very affectionate, but it is hard for them to place their affection on account of their discriminating nature. Virgo is an Earth feminine sign. It is ruled by the planet Mercury. The Lucky gem is Sapphire and Wednesday is the Lucky day.

Lucky Blessed Candles Ping and Old Cold.

72.14.44 ---- 69.39.48 ---- 617.945.735

LIBRA

(THE BALANCE)

IF YOU WERE BORN BETWEEN SEPTEMBER 23 AND OCTOBER 23

The people born under this sign are energetic, ambitious, generous and inspired. Libra people are self-reliant, seek their own way and find their own companions and occupations.

In gratifying their appetites and desires they often become reckless, the same as they do when engaged in speculation. They seek pleasure and exciting sensations and new objects to interest them, and losses and disasters mean very little to them, as they are hopeful and strong and know how to quickly recover and get back on their feet again.

Libra people are generous to a fault, and will often give away all they possess to bring happiness to others, refusing to accept anything in return for their generous impulses. They must learn to rule and dominate this power so that it will not lead them into misery and grief by bestowing too much sympathy.

Libra people do not get angry quickly, but when they do they leave nothing unsaid and as it takes them a long time to recover from a bad spell of anger they should be very careful to control their passion. They like their kind acts to be recognized by thanks or praise and should try to overcome this and do good deeds for their own sakes and without thought of reward.

When deciding important matters, Libra people should always be alone, as they are more or less subject to the positive mind of others and often go wrong when they follow the advice of others. Most Libra people have wonderful magnetic, hypnotic, and intuitive powers, but owing to their lack of faith or realization of the purer and higher realms of life they don't know how to use them to advantage.

Libra women are of a jovial, gay, happy disposition. They are fond of all places of amusement and are very popular with the opposite sex. They are not so reckless as the men of this sign, but they are apt to be very careless about money matters and with their belongings. They display much originality, and no women in the world have a keener sense of justice than Libra women.

They are quick and active in all their movements, and often impatient with the slow methods of others and sometimes become sarcastic and cutting. Libra sign is ruled by the planet Venus and the Lucky gem of this sign is Opal, Lucky day is Thursday.

Lucky Blessed Candles Pink and Old Cold.

11.27.48 ---- 62.17.53 ---- 487-961.489

SCORPIO

(THE SCORPION)
IF YOU WERE BORN BETWEEN OCTOBER 23 AND NOVEMBER 22

The name Scorpio is ominous and suggests a fatal sting. but that by no means exhausts its meaning. This is the most powerful of the twelve signs. It is a watery, feminine sign, ruled by Mars, and in all ancient symbolism the serpent stood for wisdom and physical power.

There are no more helpful people in all the world than the fully developed Scorpio people, and without them the world would not be in the position it is today. but would be in a rather sorry plight indeed.

If the people of this sign will cultivate their higher natures and train their naturally strong mental faculties, there is scarcely any undertaking in which they cannot achieve splendid success, and it is only the ignorant and violently inclined of this sign who fail. They are fond of good things of life, and have good taste in dress, are usually neat and tidy about their person, and there is no more practical or sensible set of people in all the twelve signs than the educated Scorpio.

They are very independent and seldom seek help from anyone, and as a rule what they accomplish in the world is done through their own efforts. They are always very busy and have no time to meddle with the business of others, and this is one reason why they are generally successful.

Scorpio people are inclined to be very secretive, and often their nearest friends are puzzled to know what they are going to do next. Set-backs in life are not much to them. They keep all troubles to themselves, and with their great courage they go through life overriding all obstacles.

Some of these people are very vulgar, and have a low motive for every act they perform. They will use a Friend as long as he can be used. Ile is a splendid fellow, but when he cannot be used for their personal gain and pleasure he will then be tossed away like an old garment. Yet should they later feel that they again require the service of their discarded friend, they will come to him as though nothing had happened, and gain his friendship back, as they possess much magnetic power and can often win bark the confidence of a friend no matter how shamefully they have treated him.

Scorpio people are very persistent, and indefatigable in their efforts to carry out their purposes. One thing Scorpio people must learn is that a friend in need is a friend indeed, and that one true friend is worth more than an army of pretenders. True friends are not common, for true men and women are hard to hurl in this material age.

They can be anything they choose to be, and can climb to the greatest of heights if they will but overcome their lower nature, which must be done, else it will drag them down till the soul within them dies. The women of this sign have excellent taste and match originality. Their love goes out only to the ones who are near to them.

Mars is Scorpio ruling planet, Topaz the Lucky gem and Saturday the Lucky day. Lucky Blessed Candles Yellow and Blue.
31.57.15 ---- 42.61.70 ---- 561.269.482

SAGITTARIUS

(THE ARCHER)

IF YOU WERE BORN BETWEEN NOVEMBER 22 AND DECEMBER 22

The most noted characteristics of those born under this sign are their great executive ability and the intensity of their purpose. These people are courageous, fearless and daring, and generally know how and what to aim at, and as a rule hit the mark in all matters. They can see far ahead and can easily tell at the very inception how an enterprise is going to turn out. When they rely on their own judgment they are usually successful, but when they act upon advice from others they are sure to make mistakes. Lazy people are seldom found in this sign. They are fond of business, and their health and happiness depend upon being kept busy.

Sagittarius people, when in the employ of others, need but one telling. Tell them once and leave them alone, and they will carry out the most strenuous task. They are neat and orderly, are very careful in matters pertaining to money, are saving, but not stingy or penurious, and are seldom found without a fair amount of money. They waste neither time nor money, but make the best use of both. They do not propose to keep grinding away all their lives by improvidence. Saving with these people is a beauty, and should be practiced by all to some degree. The talents of these people are many and varied. They can turn their hands to many things, and as a rule can make money when others starve.

Sagittarius people are very positive in all they undertake, and this brings them success. They are very blunt and outspoken, and often make enemies by being so, but they feel that the truth and right hurt no man.

One of the great faults of Sagittarius people is that they expect too much of others born in less active signs, being phenomenal workers themselves. This is wrong, and they should make allowance for people who are less gifted than themselves.

The women of this sign are the finest housekeepers, and among the most devoted wives. They have a great love for children and animals, are kind, gentle, noble, generous, and have great wisdom. These women are very affectionate, and when their affection is misplaced they often resolve to make the best of their bargains and to the outside world appear to be happy, while in the home they are miserable. They attend strictly to their own affairs, and have enough of their own manifold activities to be interested in without bothering themselves with the affairs of others. They despise all who are shiftless and lazy. They are honest, and never harbor ill will or bear malice, although they never forget an injury.

People born under this sign should be exceedingly careful in the selection of life mates. For a misstep here often means a misfortune in Life. Being naturally pure in thought and high-minded, they despise anything that is low arid vulgar, and licentiousness is especially distasteful to them. They will find their most congenial mates under Gemini, Aries, and their own sign, Sagittarius.

Sagittarius sign is ruled by the planet Jupiter. The Lucky gem is Turquoise. The Lucky day is Friday.

Lucky Blessed Candles Red and Orange.

15.77.62 ---- 29.68.73 ---- 528.335.684

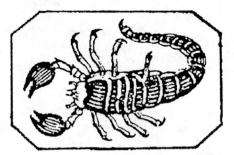

WEDDING ANNIVERSARIES

At the end of the:

First Year	Cotton
Second Year	Paper
Third Year	Leather
Fifth Year	Wooden
Seventh Year	Woolen
Tenth Year	Tin
Twelfth Year	Silk, fine linen
Fifteenth Year	Crystal
Twentieth Year	China
Twenty-fifth Year	Silver
Thirtieth Year	Pearl
Fortieth Year	Ruby
Fiftieth Year	Golden
Seventy-fifth Year	Diamond

INTERNATIONAL IMPORTS
PUBLISHER & DISTRIBUTOR OF NEW AGE BOOKS

BOOKS IN PRINT

- ❏ 70372 Black & White Magic - by Marie Laveau $6.95
- ❏ 74748 Candle Burning Magic - by Anna Riva $7.95
- ❏ 70344 Crystal Gazing 6 lessons Revised - by Dr. Ra Mayne $2.95
- ❏ 74751 Devotion to the Saints - by Anna Riva..............................$7.95
- ❏ 79969 Domination - by Anna Riva..$6.95
- ❏ 77012 Golden Secrets of Mystic Oils - by Anna Riva...................$8.95
- ❏ 70007 Guiding Light to Power & Success - by Mikhail Strabo.....$6.95
- ❏ 75969 How to Conduct a Seance - Revised by Anna Riva..........$4.95
- ❏ 77883 How to Use a Ouija Board - Michael St. Christopher........$6.95
- ❏ 77726 King Tut Dream Book $7.95
- ❏ 73952 Magic with Incense & Powders - by Anna Riva.................$7.95
- ❏ 72100 Modern Herbal Spell Book - by Anna Riva........................$6.95
- ❏ 70291 Modern Witchcraft Spell Book - Anna Riva $6.95
- ❏ 73954 Old Love Charms & Spells - Michael St. Christopher $6.95
- ❏ 76777 Powers of the Psalms - Anna Riva....................................$7.95
- ❏ 75299 Prayer Book - by Anna Riva $7.95
- ❏ 72260 Prayers to the Saints...$4.95
- ❏ 72293 Secrets of Magical Seals - by Anna Riva $6.95
- ❏ 72253 Spellcraft, Hexcraft & Witchcraft - by Anna Riva $6.95
- ❏ 73987 Spiritual Cleansing - Draja Michaharic $7.95
- ❏ 70100 Voodoo Handbook of Cult Secrets - by Anna Riva...........$6.95
- ❏ 76602 Witch's Spellcraft Revised - by Tarostar $7.95
- ❏ 77480 Your Lucky Number Forever - by Anna Riva....................$8.95

Ask for these books at a bookstore, spiritual supply store or botanica. You can also order from us. Check the boxes next to the books you have selected. Add the total. Shipping costs are $2.50 for the first book and 75¢ for each additional book. California residents add 9.75% for sales tax. Sorry no C.O.D.'S. Canada and Mexico customers shipping costs $5.00 for the first title and $1.00 for each additional book. Foreign customers shipping costs $7.00 for the first title and $1.00 for each additional book.

✂ SEND ORDER TO: WISDOM PRODUCTS
2750 S. Alameda St.
Los Angeles, CA 90058

Prices Expire JAN, 2013

NAME: _____

Address: _____

City: _____ State: _____ Zip: _____

Phone: (323) 234-3089   www.wisdomproducts.com